KU-167-376

Published by Ladybird Books Ltd.
A Penguin Company
Penguin Books Ltd, 80 Strand, London, WC2R 0RL, England
Penguin Books Australia Ltd, Camberwell, Victoria, Australia
Penguin Books (NZ) cnr Airborne and Rosedale Roads, Albany, Auckland 1310, New Zealand

2 4 6 8 10 9 7 5 3

Manufactured in Italy

www.ladybird.co.uk

Ladybird

Woody the cowboy was Andy's favourite toy. He lived in Andy's bedroom with Slinky Dog, Rex the dinosaur, Mr Potato Head, Hamm the pig, Bo Peep and all the other toys. These toys were special. When no one was around, they came to life!

One day, Woody called all the toys together. "Andy and his family are moving house soon," he told them. "That's why Andy's having his birthday party today."

The toys were worried. A birthday party meant new toys. What if Andy liked his new toys more than he liked them?

"One of us might be replaced!" groaned Rex.

"There's no need to worry," Woody promised. "Andy wouldn't do that."

As Andy unwrapped his presents, the toys waited nervously. Everything was alright until the very last parcel – a marvellous spaceman. Andy brought him up to the bedroom and left him there.

"I'm Buzz Lightyear, Space Ranger," the newcomer said, flashing his lights.

Everyone thought Buzz was wonderful. Everyone, that is, except Woody. Woody was jealous!

"You're not a Space Ranger," he sneered. "You're just a toy like the rest of us!"

SPACE RANGER
LIGHTYEAR

Suddenly, they heard barking outside and rushed to the window. Sid, the boy next door, was attacking a toy soldier. His dog, Scud, was watching excitedly.

"Sid's horrible," Rex told Buzz. "He tortures toys just for fun."

The toys watched helplessly as Sid destroyed the soldier.

As the toys went back to their places, Woody was still mad with Buzz. He thought that if he aimed the remote control car at Buzz, the new toy would fall behind the desk and be lost. But the car sped out of control, and everything went wrong – ending up with Buzz falling out of the window.

"It was an accident!" said Woody. But none of the toys would believe him.

Suddenly, Andy burst into the room. He was going to Pizza Planet and wanted to take a toy.

"I can't find Buzz, Mum," he called. "I'll have to take Woody instead."

But Buzz *did* go with them! He had fallen into a bush and leapt onto the car just as it drove away.

Pizza Planet was full of arcade games. Buzz thought one was a spaceship and crawled inside, followed by Woody.

It was crammed with toy aliens that were picked up by a claw. Woody and Buzz were horrified when they saw who had managed to grab them – it was Sid, Andy's cruel neighbour.

Back in Sid's bedroom, Woody and Buzz were terrified. They were surrounded by weird-looking mutants which Sid had made from toys he had broken. The mutants crawled closer and closer towards Woody and Buzz.

"Get back, you savages!" cried Woody. "Buzz, come on, we've got to get out of here – fast!"

They had just escaped, when Buzz heard a voice. "Come in, Buzz Lightyear," it called. "This is Star Command."

Buzz left Woody hiding in a cupboard and ran towards the voice. But it was only a television advertisement for the Buzz Lightyear toy.

Buzz was stunned. "Is it true?" he whispered. "Am I really... a toy?"

Desperate to prove he was a real Space Ranger, Buzz tried to fly. But he crashed to the floor, breaking his arm.

Woody found Buzz and took him back to Sid's room. Looking out of Sid's window, he saw his old friends in Andy's room.

"Hey guys, help!" Woody called to them, waving madly.

But the toys were angry with Woody because they thought he had hurt Buzz. "Murderer!" shouted Mr Potato Head, as Slinky Dog pulled down the blind.

Woody turned sadly away from the window – it seemed that he and Buzz were prisoners in Sid's house.

Luckily, Sid's mutant toys turned out to be friendly after all. That night, they mended Buzz's arm.

Later on, Sid burst into the room. He grabbed Buzz and tied a big rocket to his back. "I've got a surprise for you, spaceman," he sniggered. "Tomorrow I'm sending you to infinity and beyond!"

That night, Buzz was sad and gloomy. "You were right," he told Woody. "I'm not a Space Ranger. I'm just a toy."

"But being a toy is what makes you special," said Woody. "You're Andy's toy and he thinks you're great. He needs us, and we have to get back to him!"

Buzz thought for a moment. "You're right," he said at last. "Let's go!"

But it was too late! BRRRRRIINNG rang Sid's alarm clock. Sid reached out, smashed the clock and picked up Buzz.

"Today's the day, spaceman," he said. He rushed downstairs and into the garden, where he started to build a launchpad...

Woody turned to Sid's toys for help.

"Please help me save Buzz," he begged them. "He's my friend." The mutant toys smiled at Woody and nodded. Together, they worked out a plan to rescue Buzz.

Out in the garden, Sid was ready to light the fuse on Buzz's rocket. "Ten! Nine! Eight!" he counted.

Suddenly, Sid spied Woody on the ground. As he picked up the cowboy, his other toys crawled out and surrounded him. Then Woody spoke...

"AAAAAGH!" yelled Sid. "Help! These toys are alive!" Screaming, he ran into the house.

Woody and Buzz were free! They thanked the mutant toys for their help and began to make their way home. But Andy's family were just driving away, followed by the removal van!

"It's moving day!" gasped Buzz.

"There they go!" yelled Woody. "Quick! We've got to catch them!"

The two friends rushed after the van. Buzz managed to climb onto the van's back bumper. But Woody was caught by Scud, who had chased them.

"Get away!" shouted Woody, trying to free himself. Scud just growled louder...

Bravely, Buzz leapt off the bumper and fought off Scud, who ran back to his house. Now Woody was on the van – but Buzz was stranded on the road!

Woody scrambled into the removal van and found the box that contained Andy's toys. They were amazed to see him!

"Buzz is out there and he's in trouble," Woody told them. "We've got to help him!" He grabbed the remote control car and sent it speeding down the street.

"Hey!" cried Mr Potato Head. "He's trying to get rid of us like he did to Buzz! Let's get him!"

Shouting angrily, the toys threw Woody out of the van.

But a moment later, the toys' shouts turned to gasps of amazement as they saw Woody and Buzz come zooming towards them in the remote control car.

"Look! They're together!" said Rex. "Woody was telling the truth, after all."

Then, the car slowed down and stopped.

"The batteries have run down!" howled Buzz.

Woody and Buzz watched miserably as the van disappeared into the distance.

Suddenly, Buzz remembered somethi
"Woody! The rocket!" he yelled. Sid's rocket was still tied to his back!

They lit the fuse and WHOOOSH! The rocket carried them up into the sky.

Just before it exploded, Buzz pressed a button on his chest. Out popped his wings, freeing them from the rocket.

"We're flying!" laughed Woody as they soared over the van. Seconds later, they dropped gently through the sunroof of Andy's car.

Woody and Buzz were safe – and they were back with the boy who loved them.

After their adventures, Woody and Buzz became firm friends. Woody no longer felt jealous of Buzz, and the spaceman was happy to be a toy like everyone else. They all settled down together in the new house and the next few months passed happily for everyone.

Christmas came and snow fell thick and soft outside the house. Andy ran downstairs to open his beautifully wrapped Christmas presents.

Once again, the toys watched for the arrival of new toys.

"Nervous, Buzz?" asked Woody.

"No," replied Buzz. "Are you?"

"Tell me, Buzz," laughed Woody. "What could Andy possibly get that would be worse than you?"

The answer came as an excited yelp.

"Oh, no!" laughed the toys. "A PUPPY!"